All Dried

D0190940

Leslie Andrade   PJ Chan   Adam Favela   Sydni Gethner

Mariah Gorham   Maggie Gould   Nathan Gould   Daniel Levy

Ashley Paetow   Austin Paetow   Victor Serrato   Harrison Trachman

Chloe Vicino   Sara Witzel   Allie York   Jack York

For information regarding WeWrite Kids!™ Books,
WeWrite Book-Writing Workshops and products, contact:
WeWrite Company
11040 Alba Road
Ben Lomond, CA 95005
831-336-3382 • 800-295-9037 • fax: 831-336-8592

Project Coordination: Delores Palmer
WeWrite President
Illustrations: Troy Freeman
www.digitalldesigns.com
Layout & Editing: Rita Brodland
Workshop Coordinator and Facilitator
Visit us on the web at www.wewrite.net

All Dried Out
ISBN 1-57635-063-0 softcover $11.95
WeWrite Kids!™ Book #50
Ewing Irrigation
3441 E. Harbour Drive
Phoenix, AZ 85034
800.343.9464 • fax 602.437.0446 • www.ewing1.com

Project Coordination, Research, Content Accuracy:
Lacy Hyland ~ Public Relations Manager
Kelli Rangel ~ Marketing Communications Coordinator
Sarah Ellis ~ Public Relations Specialist
Graphics: Tyler Fickett, Leigh Shinn, Shawn Reed, and Nikole Sorensen
Photography: Jesse Tallman

Foreword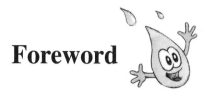

All Dried Out, the newest book in the WeWrite series, teaches children, students, parents, and teachers ways to conserve water through the escapades of a varied group of characters, and 10 year-old brother and sister twins, Jackie and Brian. The premise of the story, conceived by a group of kid co-authors, is that suddenly there is "no water."

Seeing a crisis, the group sets out through their neighborhood discovering how water is wasted, and how it can be better managed and conserved. Water is one of the Earth's most precious, non-renewable resources. It is essential to life for plants, animals, and humans. There is a finite quantity on the planet, and the amount has not changed for eons. Three percent of the Earth's water is fresh water, and two-thirds of that is tied up in glaciers and polar ice caps. Surprisingly, only one percent of all water on the planet is available to meet the needs of the world's population. As the world's population continues to grow, it puts a continually increasing strain on our fresh water supply. Different uses for water begin to compete for this limited supply. Competing uses include human health, industry, fish and wildlife, agriculture, recreation, and environmental needs.

Throughout the journey, children are encouraged to educate themselves, their parents, and others about using and managing water wisely. The examples cited in the story are techniques that students and children can put to immediate use in their daily lives, both at home, and at school.

Funded by Ewing Irrigation Products with support from the Irrigation Association Education Foundation, this book is designed to be used by teachers and parents to encourage children to properly manage our water sources. Children are invited to join the adventure as Jackie and Brian learn about proper water management and conservation. As the adventure takes them to the neighborhood grocery store, farmers market, park, golf course, and local TV station, the wasteful use of water, as well as the technologies involved in managing water, are encountered and explained. Meeting professionals in their area, they learn proper water use practices.

Readers should come away with an increased awareness that water is limited in quantity, and needs to be conserved whenever possible.

~ Brian E. Vinchesi, *Irrigation Consulting, Inc.,*
CID, CIC, CLIA, CGIA

This book is
endorsed by:

3

Chapter 1

With a sigh, mom set two plates on the table. As twins, Brian and Jackie often liked the same things… but as ten-year old kids, they were pretty picky. Their mom picked up her keys, purse, and phone saying, "Kids, I have to go run a few errands…I shouldn't be gone too long. Your dad is in the family room watching football. Try not to bother him. Be good!" The kids nodded, then turned their attention back to lunch.

"I think this is rotten," Jackie said as she examined her food.

Before he even looked, a smile spread across Brian's face. "Cool, then we don't have to eat it!"

"Seriously Brian…look at it!" Jackie's lip curled in disgust.

Brian stopped to look. "Whoa, did Mom replace our food with the dog's food?" His eyes grew wide as he stared at the dried up food. "This is gross."

Suddenly, tiny eyes popped open on the broccoli. Immediately, the broccoli jerked itself out from under a piece of chicken. "Get off of me, you big, fat chicken leg!"

"Hey, what's your problem?" the chicken leg snapped back, opening its eyes and scowling.

Brian's jaw dropped. He looked at his sister and whispered, "Did that just happen?" Jackie's eyes were huge. "I think I'm insane," he said.

"No, Brian—I saw it, too." Jackie was thoughtful. "Maybe Mom put 'alive' powder on your food."

"Now THAT'S crazy," said Brian.

"I hate you, Clucky," the broccoli exclaimed. The chicken leg jumped up. "So?" he said. "Bring it on, Bonito!"

The chicken leg and broccoli began wrestling, causing quite a commotion. "Oh, please," said a sleepy voice from the other side of Brian's plate. "Will you two STOP fighting? I'm TRYING to sleep here."

Brian and Jackie shifted their attention to the shriveled up strawberry. "Uh, excuse me?" Jackie stammered. "Who are you?"

"My name is…" she began, but Bonito interrupted. "Her name is…Umm…." The strawberry sighed. "My name is not 'Umm,' my name is Chelsea, and I'm very tired. Will you two please stop fighting and be quiet?"

The cup by Jackie's plate opened its eyes and rattled a little bit. Chelsea looked over at it. "Slurpy Ella, do you have any water? My muscles are weak and I feel so worn down and tired."

The cup shook her head, "No," she said sadly, "I'm completely empty."

"Mom must've forgotten the water," Jackie explained. "Can I take you to the kitchen and fill you up, Slurpy Ella?" The cup agreed. Jackie carefully picked up the talking cup, holding it as far away as possible. She began walking toward the sink, her eyes big and her face white.

"Well if you hold me like that, you're going to drop me!" the cup whined.

Jackie kept her arm stretched out. "You're a talking cup. What do you expect?" Jackie replied. They got to the sink and Jackie tried to turn on the faucet. "No water," Jackie called to Brian. "Now we know why the cup is empty."

The cup sighed. Brian hurried over to see for himself. He tried the faucet, but nothing happened. All he could do was shrug his shoulders. From the table they heard voices.

"No water? We're DYING!" The food was beginning to panic.

Brian motioned to Jackie to pick up the cup, and they all went back to the table. "It'll be okay," Jackie tried to reassure them. But she wasn't so sure herself. "Do you think we should ask Dad if he knows what's going on?"

"While he's watching football? Probably not the best idea." Brian's stomach grumbled. "Can I eat you?" Brian asked the chicken leg, poking him with a fork.

"Don't even think about it, dude!" cried Clucky.

He jumped up with his fists in the air, ready to fight.

"Why would you want to eat Clucky, anyway? He's all dried up and nasty," Chelsea said. Clucky dropped his fists and gave Chelsea a dirty look.

"Stop fighting!" Jackie yelled. "It's FOOD, Brian. I can't believe you're scared of it."

"I'm not scared of it," Brian sneered at his sister, ready to pick a fight.

But the strawberry interrupted the twins' argument. "Can someone PLEASE get me some water?" Chelsea said dramatically. "I'm so weak."

"Ay-ay-ay," Bonito exclaimed, slapping his hand to his dry, green forehead.

"Enough," Jackie said sternly. "We have bigger problems, like no water."

"You said it, sister," Bonito agreed. "Umm, I'm sorry," he said, looking at the strawberry.

Chelsea just sighed.

Chapter 2

"I'm going to call Andee. Let's see if we're the only ones with no water," Jackie said. She dialed the phone. Ring, ring! "Hey, Andee—I know this is a strange question, but do you have any water at your house?"

"I don't know, let me go check." Andee set down the phone and checked her faucet. Nothing. She came back to the phone and told Jackie. "That's so bizarre! We don't have any water either. Maybe we should check the news to see what is going on." Jackie agreed.

"Andee doesn't have water, either," Jackie told Brian. "She suggested that we turn on the TV and see if there is anything on the news."

"I'm on it," Brian answered. He turned on the little TV in the kitchen just in time to see a flashing screen and hear beeping noises.

"This is breaking news. We are LIVE on location where people are discovering that there is NO WATER." The serious newsman pushed his microphone in front of several surprised-looking people. "What do YOU think?"

"I think somebody better figure something out pretty quick. This is serious!" said one man. Another person agreed, "It's a huge problem."

"There you have it," said the newsman. "A water shortage is leaving many people in the area high and dry."

Brian clicked off the TV. "Oh, snap," said Jackie. "What now?"

"Let's go to the store to BUY water!" cried Clucky.

Bonito's eyes lit up. He wanted water, but more importantly, he knew that at the store he could look for his long-lost love, BonitaLita. "To the Broccoli-Mobile!" exclaimed Bonito, punching his fist into the air like a superhero. He grabbed a piece of Swiss cheese and flung it around his shoulders like a cape.

"Do you mean our bicycle basket?" asked Jackie as she and Brian carefully scooped up the food and cup.

"I mean, it's a green bike but...."

"Let it go, Jackie," Brian whispered. "He's on a roll."

"I'm going to go ask Dad if we can go on a bike ride to the store. It's not very far—and we've done it before.

I don't think he'll care." Jackie went to get permission, and came back quickly with an 'okay' from Dad.

Brian placed Clucky and Chelsea in the bicycle basket. Jackie carefully put the cup in the corner, but Bonito jumped

from her hand to the front of the basket. The children climbed on the two-person bike and began pedaling.

Bonito let loose with a battle cry, "Dun-dun-da-DUN!" His cheese cape was flying behind him.

Clucky wasn't impressed. "That cape is MINE," he muttered, yanking at the cheese.

"Cut it out, you crazy chicken leg!" They started wrestling again, while the cup pulled back further into the corner, looking worried.

"I'm trying to sleep, you guys!" said a frustrated Chelsea.

"Umm..." said Bonito.

"Oh, leave me alone," sighed Chelsea.

Bonito climbed back to the front of the basket. Clucky took one last swipe at his cape and pulled a little bit off.

It fell to the ground, and as they bicycled away, they could hear a little voice saying, "I'm melting! Mellltttiiinng!"

Very soon, they pulled up in front of the grocery store. "BonitaLita! BonitaLita! Where are you, my love?" The superhero broccoli hopped out of the bicycle basket and jumped up and down on the automatic doormat, trying to open the door.

"Oh please let me in," he muttered to himself. Brian stepped up and the door finally opened. "To the produce section!" he shouted, with his fist in the air.

Jackie picked up the cup and the sleepy strawberry. "Come on, you two...let's go find some water!" she said to them. "Brian, you take Clucky and go find Bonito." He nodded.

Slurpy Ella was nervous. "I hope we find water. I feel so empty inside!" As soon as they turned the corner to the drink aisle, Jackie could see a big, open area. There was no water on the shelves anywhere.

"Oh no, it's too late," she said. "What are we going to do now?"

Chelsea opened her sleepy eyes. "Oh, no. Oh, say it isn't so! Well, maybe there's some water up on the highest shelf. Hold me up and I'll look."

Jackie lifted the strawberry. Chelsea held on to Jackie's hand for dear life. She was scared, but trying to be brave. "Whee!" she said in an unconvincing voice. After a moment, she called down to Jackie and Slurpy Ella, "I don't see anything! Can I come down now?"

Jackie slowly lowered Chelsea. They all looked depressed. "I guess we should find everyone else," Slurpy Ella said softly. They began walking toward the produce aisle.

Meanwhile, Brian was carrying the chicken leg firmly in his fist, keeping it as far away as possible. "Why are you holding me so tight?" Clucky asked. "It hurts! When I get down from here, you're dead meat." "Give it a rest, chicken," Brian muttered.

From a couple of aisles away, Jackie, Chelsea and Slurpy Ella heard Brian and Clucky fighting.

"Oh, THERE they are," said Slurpy Ella. "It sounds like Clucky is mad."

Chelsea rolled her eyes. "Not again," she moaned as they walked over to the produce section.

Suddenly they heard a whimpering voice behind them. "Ay, BonitaLita! I'm about to cry." He turned to the little group. "I cannot find my sweet BonitaLita," he shook his head sadly.

Brian and Jackie looked at each other. Then everyone looked down feeling sorry for the broccoli. But quickly, Jackie's face lit up. "I know! The Farmer's Market! Let's go to the Farmer's Market. There is ALWAYS fresh produce there!" Everyone agreed. Bonito perked up immediately.

EveryBODY Needs Water!

Water is the single most abundant substance in the human body. A person can live several days without food, but just a few days without water! Like air, water is essential to life. Because water is so important, health and nutrition experts recommend at lease two liters of water each day. This makes bottled water a convenient way to help ensure that enough water is consumed at home, school, or wherever you may be.

"You'd better call Dad and let him know where we're going," Brian told Jackie.

Jackie sneered at her brother, "What happened to your dialing fingers? I'm not interrupting football. You call!"

Clucky threw up his arms. "One of you had better call. Broccoli-Boy is getting ready to leave without us."

"To the Farmer's Market! Dun-dun-da-DUN!" Bonito declared, leading the group out to the bicycle with his fist high in the air once again, acting like a superhero.

Brian smiled at the excited veggie. "I'll call Dad."

Chapter 3

"Faster, faster! We must find BonitaLita," cried Bonito, hanging on to the front of the bicycle basket, his torn cheese cape flapping in the wind.

"What about the water?" asked a worried Slurpy Ella. The kids were pedaling as fast as they could. Clucky, Chelsea, and the cup were all bouncing around crazily from the bumpy ride.

Very soon, they got to the Farmer's Market.

"Wow, all this food looks bad, too," Brian said. "It's all dried up and rotten."

Clucky looked around and muttered, "I hate my life. Not another chicken leg in sight."

"I guess these fruits and vegetables didn't get enough water, either," said Jackie, looking around at the pale and sorry-looking produce.

Bonito saw a bunch of broccoli and jumped out of the basket to go look for his lost love. It didn't take him long to find her. "BonitaLita!" he cried as he approached the shriveled broccoli.

"I'm here," a faint voice called softly. Bonito's heart jumped out of his chest as he struggled to reach

BonitaLita. She was withered and twitching.

Bonito turned and shouted, "Brian! Come here. Help! I found her. I found BonitaLita!" He gently snuggled against her, looking at her lovingly. She managed a weak smile.

Brian hurried over and picked them up, "Don't worry, Bonito. We'll take care of her. We'll take care of you both."

Jackie and the rest joined them. "I'm so glad you found her," she said to Bonito. "My name is Jackie," she said to the little piece of broccoli. "This is my brother, Brian."

She introduced the strawberry, the cup, and the chicken leg. "Your husband has been searching for you." Jackie explained what was going on. "We'll do our best to help you, BonitaLita," she said, trying to sound reassuring.

Slurpy Ella caught sight of something. "Hey, did anyone notice those fruits and vegetables over there? They look great."

"What in the world is going on?" asked Clucky.

"Well, let's go ask," said Brian.

The group walked over to the nice-looking produce stand. They saw a sign that read Farmer Brown's Fresh Produce. A woman at the stand was putting some bright red chili peppers in a bag for a customer. After the customer paid for the peppers, the farmer thanked her, and said goodbye. Jackie walked up to the stand and said, "Excuse me, but are you Farmer Brown?"

"I certainly am," she said, smiling at the kids. "Can I help you?"

"I hope so," said Jackie. "So much of the food here at the Farmer's Market looks bad, but yours looks really good. We were curious, why do your fruits and vegetables look so healthy?"

Farmer Brown looked around at the other stands and said, "Well, some of the produce looks like it may have been over-watered. Too much water, or watering at the wrong time of day, can cause fungus to grow and can damage the plants. But most of the produce looks wilted, dry, and not fully developed. That usually means not enough water."

"I know WE don't have enough water right now," Brian said. "In fact, we don't have ANY. But plants don't grow overnight—and we HAD water yesterday. So that doesn't explain why this produce looks all dried out."

Brian was pointing at some of the other produce stands. "But yours looks good. Did you have more water than everyone else?"

Farmer Brown explained that she didn't have any MORE water than anyone else—she just used the water that she DID have more carefully. "It's called 'Water Conservation,' and it isn't that hard to do—but it IS

something that needs to be planned carefully."

She explained, "To be honest, I don't have a real farm, just a very big garden. I love growing things, and I'm always looking for ways to grow bigger and better fruits and vegetables."

She looked around at the other produce stands. "I'm sure that everyone here tries to do their best, but sometimes they have older equipment, or just old-fashioned ways of doing things. We've learned a lot in the last few years, and lots of terrific new things have been developed to help. Water conservation is important. Maybe you kids can help spread the word!"

"Water conservation," Jackie said thoughtfully. "I guess it just seems like we'll always have enough water. Why would we run out? Why should we be careful about saving water?"

"We don't have any water NOW," Brian pointed out. "It's a natural resource, like trees and stuff. We learned that in school, remember?"

"And we need to protect our natural resources," Jackie agreed. "I just never thought we'd run out of water so fast!"

Brian raised one eyebrow and looked at his sister sideways. "Oh c'mon, Jackie. You know we're not REALLY all out of water."

"How do you know?" Jackie argued. "We might be! You don't know everything." But then looking at the dried out food and the empty cup, she decided not to pick a fight with her twin. "Let's just go home and see if the water is back on, okay?"

21

Chapter 4

Brian and Jackie put everyone into the basket. "There, is everyone comfortable?" asked Jackie. Chelsea nodded. Bonito held BonitaLita lovingly in his arms.

Slurpy Ella was so worn out from being thirsty that she almost fainted. "Water…we just need some water," Chelsea said weakly.

Clucky climbed to the back of the basket so he could see Brian. He was peeking around Jackie and shaking his fist at Brian saying, "You're mine. Just you wait and see!" Brian shrugged.

The kids were riding their bicycle past some businesses. Water was all over the sidewalk. "Look out!" called Jackie as the bike splashed through the puddles. "There's some wasted water," she said. "We should teach THEM about water conservation."

"I guess they think the sidewalk needs to be watered. And the driveway, too!" Brian looked back as they rode past. "I bet if they just adjusted their sprinklers so the water only hit the grass, they wouldn't waste so much water."

"Ay-ay-ay!" cried Bonito. "If only WE had that water!"

"But look over there," said Slurpy Ella, who was now awake and peeking out of the basket. "All those flowers are dying."

"Indeed," sighed BonitaLita. "Such a waste! Too much water here, and not enough water there." Bonito patted her hand.

They rode along in silence. Clucky had given up trying to pick a fight with Brian. Slurpy Ella was clunking around in the basket, wishing for a drink. Chelsea had rolled over by BonitaLita and the two were getting to know each other. Bonito just stared out of the basket, still holding on to BonitaLita. After a while, they saw a nice, big, green area.

"Is that a park?" asked Jackie.

"I think it's a golf course," Brian said. "Wow. It's beautiful! THEY must know something about water conservation."

"Let's stop and ask," suggested Jackie. They turned down a path and started riding through the lush, green golf course toward a building surrounded by shrubs and flowers. "That must be the clubhouse. Maybe we can find someone to talk to there."

The group steered their green bike toward the little building. Brian went inside to ask who was responsible for keeping the golf course so green and

neat. "That would be the Superintendent," the man behind the counter told Brian. "He's right outside."

It didn't take long for the kids to find someone checking a hose around the corner of the building. They carefully parked the bike nearby so Clucky, Chelsea, and the rest could all hear.

"Excuse me, but are you the Superintendent?" asked Jackie.

"I sure am," he said with a smile. "Did you need something?" he asked.

"Not exactly," said Brian. "We just wanted to ask you a few questions."

"No problem. What did you want to know?" replied the man.

Jackie asked, "What all does a superintendent do?"

"Well, I take care of the grounds--all the land and everything on it. Most of all, I make sure that everything is green and neat and ready for people to play golf," he answered.

"But why does your golf course look so good?" asked Brian. "Most of the grass and trees and flowers and stuff in this neighborhood look pretty bad. Do you have more water than everyone else?"

"No, I really don't. But the people who planned this golf course put a lot of thought into it. They installed special sprinklers that use less water. And they planned for natural areas where water will drain, and where we can get water, like that pond over there." The Superintendent pointed to a quiet, little pond with

25

a fountain in the middle. "It's a lot more complicated than it looks, keeping a golf course beautiful." The Superintendent was obviously proud.

Clucky let out a little whistle. "Whew. Sweet," he said quietly. He wanted to see the fountain up close, so he began climbing out of the bicycle basket.

The Superintendent didn't seem to notice the talking chicken leg. "The watering systems are on timers," he explained.

"I make sure to adjust the timers so that the sprinklers run early in the morning when the water won't evaporate."

"And so that the golfers don't get wet!" joked Brian.

"That too." The friendly Superintendent smiled. "We also have rain sensors."

"What is a 'rain sensor'? Some sort of thing that tells you when it's about to rain?" asked Brian.

Know WHEN to WATER

Did you know you can lose as much as 30 percent of water to evaporation by watering midday? The Irrigation Association says to water your lawn when the sun is low or down, winds are calm, and temperatures are cool—between the evening and early morning—to reduce the evaporation rate.

"Well, sort of. A rain sensor doesn't predict the rain, but it can tell when rain is coming down. Then it tells the sprinklers that they don't need to run. That way, we don't waste water. We let Mother Nature water our grass when it's raining."

"That's a great idea!" exclaimed Jackie. "I wonder if we could have one of those at our house?"

"Of course you could," said the Superintendent. "In fact, I have a rain sensor installed at my own house. It works great, and it has really made a difference in my water bill. I also use drip irrigation at home, just like we do here at the clubhouse."

While the Superintendent was talking to the twins, Clucky began his adventure to investigate the pond with the fountain. Bonito was watching anxiously from the bicycle basket. "Be careful, you crazy chicken leg!" he said in a harsh whisper.

But it was too late. Clucky was rolling cheerfully toward the pond. Bonito hurried to the other side of the basket to get Jackie or Brian's attention.

The Superintendent was explaining, "Drip irrigation is a really great way to save water. It uses a tube that runs just under the surface of the ground in landscaping, like flowers and shrubs. Little pieces called 'emitters' are placed in the tube right next to each of the plants that need to be watered. Each emitter lets out just enough water for each plant."

"I guess different plants need different amounts of water," Jackie said thoughtfully. Just then she saw Bonito waving frantically. She didn't want to be rude, so she tried to make her way to the bike unnoticed.

Clucky was still rolling around in the soft grass, making his way toward the pond.

"That's right," the Superintendent continued. "The emitters keep us from over-watering or under-watering each plant. So, not only does it save water, but it keeps

them healthy."

"But why is it called 'drip' irrigation?" asked Brian.

"Because the water comes out in drops through each emitter," he explained. "It drips out. Understand?"

From the bicycle basket, Slurpy Ella clinked a little.

Save Water, Drip by Drip

The Superintendent is right-drip irrigation saves water! This irrigation method consumes up to 70 percent less water by simply applying water directly to the roots of plants, preventing evaporation and runoff.

She knew about drips from being around the faucet. She wasn't paying a bit of attention to Clucky's silly antics.

"It makes sense to me!" Jackie said hurriedly. Brian nodded in agreement. "Well, thanks for your help, Sir! We'd better be moving along now."

Brian looked at her quizzically. Jackie was motioning toward the bicycle basket with her eyes and a tilt of her head. Brian realized that something was going on, so he quickly thanked the Superintendent.

"Happy to be of help," he said, tipping his hat to the kids then returning to his work.

Slurpy Ella was excited. "I know all about drips!" she said. "Just a little drop of water comes out at a time, but it happens over and over and over and over..."

"Yes, yes," Bonito interrupted. "We all know about drips," he said, shooting a glance at Clucky still laughing and rolling around on the grass.

"Clucky!" Jackie scolded. "What would we do if you rolled into the pond and sunk to the bottom?"

She picked up Clucky and carried him back to the bicycle basket.

"I was just having some fun," the chicken leg said with a scowl. "Can't a chicken leg have any fun around here?"

Bonito ignored him, thrusting his right arm in the air like a superhero again. "Dun-dun-da-DUN!" he said, wrapping his other arm around BonitaLita. "The search for water continues!" BonitaLita smiled at her hero.

Chapter 5

On their way home, the kids rode past the grocery store. "I wonder when they'll get more water," Slurpy Ella said longingly.

Suddenly they heard a SQUISH! They heard a little voice say, "Ow…ow…ow…Hey!…ow…I'm down here!...ow," over and over again. Clucky laughed to himself as he realized that they had run over the piece of cheese from Bonito's torn cape and it was stuck to the tire.

"Hey Bonito, want your cape back?" Clucky asked sarcastically.

"As a matter of fact I do, Cluck-boy!" said Bonito. Clucky rolled his eyes, but Brian and Jackie stopped the bike, picked up the piece of cheese, and returned it to Bonito, much to his delight.

BonitaLita smiled at her husband. "Ignore Clucky, my love. He's just a sad and lonely chicken leg," she said. Everyone in the basket agreed. Clucky crossed his arms and threw himself down in a corner. "Hmmff," he snorted.

After a while they started seeing lots of houses.
"Hey, Jackie—did you notice how bad some of these
yards look?"

"I sure did. Look at Mr. Gruffington's yard," she said,
pointing at a particularly sorry-looking lawn.

"Man, it looks more like a lake!" cried Brian. "No
wonder...look! Mr. Gruffington left his hose running."

They stopped the bike. Bonito slapped his hand to his forehead. "Ay-ay-ay," he said.

"What a waste! We could use some of that!" Chelsea exclaimed. "We really ought to tell him."

"Take me!" Clucky demanded. "I'll give him a piece of my mind!"

"I'll take you," said Jackie as she picked up the chicken leg. "But let ME do the talking." Jackie carried Clucky to the front door. *Knock-knock-knock!*

It took a long time, but finally a man wearing an old bathrobe answered the door. "Yeah? What do you want?" he asked. He seemed annoyed.

"Mr. Gruffington, did you know that you left your hose running?" Jackie asked.

"I did?" he asked, as he looked past them into the yard. "I'll be sure to take care of that in a few seconds. Or minutes. Or hours," he said dryly. Then he slammed the door in their faces.

"How rude!" Jackie thought to herself. Jackie knocked on the door again. Mr. Gruffington opened the door just a little bit. "Sir, you really should shut that hose off now. We are in the middle of a water shortage and you're wasting water…" she began to explain. But he just slammed the door again without saying a word.

"Why even ask him?" Clucky questioned. "He's not going to do it. Let me at him!" Jackie just shook her head at the chicken leg.

"I'm tho thowwy," said a small, gurgly voice. "I can'd thtop mythelf."

"Huh? Who's that?" asked Clucky, looking around.

"It's the hose!" Jackie cried. Everyone in the basket scooted over to look at the hose, who was curled on the ground with water gushing from his mouth.

Without thinking Clucky sprang into action. "I'm on it," he said with authority. He jumped from Jackie's hand, and in one quick movement, wedged himself onto the end of the hose, slowing the flow of water.

"Ew!" the hose gurgled. "Ged oudda my mouf, you tathe bad!" The poor hose could barely talk.

"Get a hold of yourself, Clucky," Brian said. "You're going to get all soggy."

"Ugh…I can't, I'm stuck!" yelled an embarrassed Clucky.

"Well, we have to get you out of there—I'll turn off the water," offered Brian. He ran to the faucet and turned it off. Jackie pulled the mushy chicken leg out of the water.

The hose breathed a sigh of relief. "Sweet!" he said. "Thanks! My name is Homer, and I am SO grateful. That water has been pouring out of my mouth for a LONG time. I can breathe much easier now. Thank you, thank you, thank you!"

"Sure, Homer," Jackie said. She placed Clucky back in the basket.

"You smell like a wet dog," declared Bonito. "Ew!"

Chelsea moved closer to the dripping chicken leg, poking him softly with her foot. "He's so…soggy. And I'm so dry. It's not fair." She tried to get close to him to soak up some of his wetness, but he scowled at her and scooted away. "You're all yucky and muddy, anyway,"

she said. "This whole yard is a gross, muddy mess."

Bonito caught sight of a small, drooping rose bush with only one blossom. "Oh no! Look at that beautiful rose! Her petals are falling off. She seems so soggy and sad. We must help her!"

The wilted rose tried to lift her face, but her head was too heavy. "Oh, please. Can you help me? I am so over-watered."

36

"What is your name, young rose?" asked BonitaLita.

"My name is Gloria. I'm wilting. I don't think I will last much longer," she said weakly.

Bonito flipped his superhero cheese cape over his shoulder. "I, Bonito, will save you—whatever it takes: life, or death," exclaimed the heroic broccoli.

Clucky rolled his eyes. "Oh, what EVER," he grumbled.

Slurpy Ella rattled a bit in the basket. "Maybe I could help. If you dig up Gloria, I can hold her and keep her safe until she can be planted somewhere else."

"That's a wonderful idea, Slurpy Ella," Jackie said happily. "But we can't just TAKE a flower from someone's yard." Jackie looked at the front door of the house and sighed. "Mr. Gruffington isn't very friendly, but I'm going to ask, anyhow." She bravely walked to the front door and asked the grumpy man if it was okay if she took the dying flower from his front yard.

"Take it. What do I care?" he grumbled.

Jackie thanked him, and went back to the flower and told her the good news. "You're coming with us!" Jackie packed up some extra dirt around Gloria's roots and placed her carefully in the cup. Slurpy Ella didn't say anything, but inside she was happy. She finally felt like she was helping.

Everyone in the group introduced themselves to Gloria, explaining what they had been

Water Right

Over-watering is just as bad as under-watering. It not only wastes your money, but it prevents plants from getting the oxygen they need, and puts them in danger of disease. It also causes pollution by allowing fertilizers and pesticides to run off into creeks, lakes, and oceans.

doing. Once she was settled in, it was time to go. Homer the hose wanted to go, too, but Brian explained that if they took him along, it would be stealing. The hose was disappointed, but he understood. Chelsea winked at the hose, who was waving his head to say goodbye.

"Adios, amigo!" declared Bonito. "Good luck with your water problem!" The kids climbed back on the bike and started to pedal again. But they didn't get very far.

Chapter 6

The kids had just started riding away when they heard another cry.

"Help me!" said a scratchy voice.

The kids stopped the bike immediately. "Did you hear that?" asked Brian. "Did that shrub just talk?"

Jackie nodded. "I think so," she said quietly.

"Keep going," Clucky said flatly. "This basket is FULL."

Gloria tried to lift her head. "Oh, Clucky. We should help him. We can't just leave him there!"

"What's wrong with you, little shrub?" Brian asked.

The crunchy little shrub could barely talk. "I'm so dry…so very, very dry. Somebody's not watering me."

Everyone looked at each other. They knew how the poor shrub felt. But before they could say anything, they heard a voice from the other side of the driveway.

"Maybe I can help!" The kids turned to see Homer snaking across the lawn.

"Homer, what are you doing here?" asked Jackie.

"I'm sorry—it's just that…this is my neighbor, Scrub. I think I can help him. Get my hat, it's over by the faucet."

Brian hurried to the faucet and found a squeeze-trigger nozzle. He held it up, "Is this what you mean?"

"Yes, that's it!" Homer shouted. "Bring it over! Just twist it on to my head and then you can control me better."

Brian brought the nozzle to the hose.

"OK now…stay still." He screwed the nozzle on to the end of the hose. *Squeak, squeak, squeak!* The nozzle was rusty from lying in the water.

"Someone turn on the water," Brian said, holding the hose, ready to spray. Jackie ran to the faucet.

She gave Brian a 'thumbs up.' He squeezed the nozzle, and the water came out and showered the shrub.

"Ahhh…that feels nice," Scrub declared. "I like it. I feel better already!"

"What about me?" asked the lawn. It was yellow and brown, and looked pretty sad. "I need some water, too."

"Yes, please help Mr. Green Blades. He's my friend," said Scrub the shrub. Brian turned the water toward the lawn. "How's that, Blades?" Scrub asked happily. The lawn drank quickly, glad that he and Scrub finally had water.

"May I have some water, too?" Chelsea asked. "And some for Bonito and his wife. We're all thirsty!"

Brian adjusted the hose nozzle to a light sprinkle and gave them all a drink. "I don't know why I didn't think

40

of this before," Brian said.

A still-soggy Clucky looked at Jackie. "We need to let this homeowner know that he needs to take care of his yard," he said with a determined voice.

Brian looked up. "This is Mr. Ruminate's house."

Jackie picked up the chicken leg and walked up to the front door. "Don't say anything, Clucky," Jackie warned. "You might scare Mr. Ruminate."

"Fine," the chicken leg agreed, still scowling.

Ding-Dong! The door opened. "Who rang my bell?" boomed an angry voice.

"I did, Mr. Ruminate. It's your neighbor, Jackie. I need to speak to you about something."

"I don't want any cookies," the man grumbled.

He started to close the door, but Jackie blocked it with her foot, then smiled sweetly. "I'm not selling anything, Mr. Ruminate," she said. "I just want to talk to you about your lawn."

Be Prepared for an Emergency

If a hurricane, earthquake, or other disaster hits your community, you may not have access to water, similar to what happened to Jackie and Brian. In case of an emergency, store a total of at least one gallon per person, per day. You should store at least a two-week supply of water for each member of your family.

"You crazy girl. What…what are you doing with a chicken leg?" he asked.

Clucky got mad and started to shake himself out of Jackie's grasp. Mr. Ruminate just stared. He couldn't believe that a little neighbor girl with a piece of chicken was trying to teach him about how to take care of his yard.

Jackie pulled Clucky closer to her, holding him with both hands. "I'm sorry, Sir. It's just that, well, we don't have ANY water at our house. We've been all over trying to find out what is wrong. We've learned about something called 'water conservation.' It doesn't mean that you never water your lawn. It's just a lot of good ideas to help save water, and at the same time, have a healthy, beautiful lawn and garden."

After a minute he shook his head. "Okay, Jackie. I'm listening," he said.

Brian guided the bike up the driveway, and the kids talked to Mr. Ruminate about water conservation. Their neighbor actually listened. He finally said, "You kids are much smarter than I would've thought. I don't understand why you're holding a chicken leg, but what you're saying makes good sense."

He looked out at his front yard. "I don't like how it looks when it's all dried out. But Mr. Gruffington here is always watering his yard, and it doesn't look good, either. I'll talk to him. If I water more and he waters less—and we both practice water conservation—our neighborhood will look a lot better."

"And it will be good for the whole community. The whole planet, even!" Jackie said happily. They thanked Mr. Ruminate and got back on the bike.

Chapter 7

"Okay everyone, we really need to go home now," Jackie said. "I told Dad we wouldn't be gone very long." As the kids were pedaling the bike, Gloria was drooping toward Chelsea.

"Do you feel any better yet?" Chelsea asked.

"Well, I…" she started.

Bonito interrupted. "Umm…"

"My name is Chelsea, Broccoli-Man! Get it straight." Chelsea was obviously feeling stronger after drinking some water.

"I was just going to say that it will take a while for Gloria to dry out. Give her time." Bonito just shrugged and went back to his lovely wife.

Chelsea turned her attention back to the wilted rose. "Is there anything I can do for you?" she asked.

Gloria managed a smile. "I'm just so grateful for everything you guys are doing—especially you, Slurpy Ella. I'm feeling better already."

Slurpy Ella was feeling better, too. She blushed.

"We're home!" called Jackie.

Brian climbed off the bicycle and shook his legs. "Good thing, too. I'm about worn out!"

"I'm going to go check and see if there's any water," said Jackie.

Brian looked at all his little friends. "Wait here," he said. He ran inside and got a plate to hold Clucky, Chelsea, Bonito, and BonitaLita. "Can you come inside Gloria?" he asked the rose. She nodded yes. Brian picked up Slurpy Ella and Gloria, and then carried them all inside.

Jackie was standing at the sink. "Still nothing," she said. "What are we going to do?"

Brian set the plate and cup on the table, and he and Jackie sat down. "You know what I don't get?" asked a still-soggy Clucky. "Some of the places we saw today DID have water, and lots of it. I mean, look at me!"

"That is true," Bonito said thoughtfully. "It is a mystery."

"Clucky is right," Brian said. "Some places had water, and some didn't. We need to figure out why."

> ### YOU Can Make a Difference!
>
> Did you know there are hundreds of water conservation programs kids can get involved in? You can be a star by making a difference in your community—adopt a watershed or simply tell other kids about how to conserve water. Remember, every drop counts!

Jackie nodded. "Maybe we should check the news again." She found the remote control and turned on the television. After a few minutes, another news flash was announced.

"We're here at a local grocery store where hundreds of gallons of water have just been delivered." The reporter

45

stopped a woman to interview her.

"That's MOM!" the twins said at exactly the same time, grabbing each other's arms. "Dad! Switch the TV to the news…Mom is on!" They ran into the family room where their dad had just changed the channel.

"Shhhh…" Jackie whispered. "Mom's going to talk!" The kids were glued to the TV.

The reporter was very serious. Mom looked a little nervous standing near the television camera. "It took a while to find where the water line was broken. The underground pipes are quite old. But once the break was found, repair began immediately." The man nudged Mom.

"Standing by, I have a woman whose water has been turned off since very early this morning. Ma'am—I see that you're buying water now. Can you tell us what you're thinking?"

With a microphone in front of her, Mom came to life. "As soon as I realized that the water was not working, I came to the store to buy a temporary supply. But I guess I wasn't the only one with that idea." Some people in the background applauded.

Mom continued, "This store was already out. The store manager told many of us that he already had an emergency delivery on the way. I ran a few other errands, and thank goodness by the time I returned here, the store DID have water to sell. It's easy to forget how much we depend on water—until we don't have any."

"Indeed," agreed the reporter. "The city tells us that repairs will be made by sometime tomorrow.

46

But meanwhile, several water lines that are connected to this main line have been shut down. So even though the break may not be in your neighborhood, you might be affected."

The news went back to the main station, where the announcer began listing which areas were without water. They also showed tips on what to do when your water supply is low.

When it was over, Brian looked at Jackie. "Water conservation. That's what they were talking about. But we should be doing that ALL of the time."

"Everyone should!" exclaimed Jackie. She looked back at the television. "Wow. Mom was on TV. That was awesome!"

"My wife is famous," Dad laughed. "Now if only she could play football!" The kids giggled and went back to the kitchen where the plate full of food and the cup had been watching the little TV.

"If I had been on television, I would've told everyone about how to conserve water," declared Bonito. He was standing with both hands on his hips, looking every bit like a superhero.

"We need to teach everyone what we learned today," Chelsea agreed.

Gloria added, "Not just about wasting water, but using it wisely." Slurpy Ella smiled proudly.

Everyone agreed.

Chapter 8

When Mom got home, Jackie and Brian rushed outside to help her carry in the groceries and extra gallons of water. "We saw you on TV!" they yelled.

"That was so cool, Mom," said Brian.

"Were you nervous?" asked Jackie.

Mom smiled. "Well, I was a little nervous. But it just so happens that I knew the television reporter. Your Dad and I went to high school with him! He told me to just relax and talk to the camera as if I were talking to my friends. That made it easier."

"Wow!" Jackie looked at Brian, and then looked at the plate with Clucky, Chelsea, Bonito and BonitaLita, and Slurpy Ella with Gloria. An idea was beginning to form in her head. "You know a television star? That's way cool."

After the kids helped their mom put the groceries away, Jackie pulled Brian into the living room near the plate with their friends. "Are you thinking what I'm thinking?" she asked.

"If you're thinking we should get her autograph…" Brian began.

Clucky jumped up and threw his hands in the air. "Don't you get it, Brian? This is our chance!"

"Exactly," Jackie agreed. "We need a way to reach lots of people to teach them about water conservation. Mom knows someone at the television station." She put both of her hands out, trying to get Brian to make the connection.

Suddenly Brian cracked a smile. "Of course! It's perfect!"

Chelsea was plumping up, batting her eyelashes.

"I can be a TV STAR!" she declared.

"Umm…WE can be stars," Bonito corrected, patting his wife on the hand. She smiled.

The kids decided that they would need to tell their Mom and Dad about everything that had happened, starting with the talking food. "Mom, Dad—you'd better sit down," they said.

Once they had explained it all, they introduced their parents to the food and the cup. "Okay," Mom said, "this is pretty weird, but it almost makes sense, too."

The kids then went on to tell their parents about the hose, the shrub, and the lawn. "See?" explained Jackie. "It's all about the water. Too much, not enough…we need to teach people what we've learned about water conservation."

Dad winked at Mom, and said, "I think I have an idea of how we could help." The twins' mom knew just what her husband was thinking.

Mom smiled. "So, would you kids like to meet our

friend at the television station? He might be able to help."

"Let's go!" they said. The kids carefully gathered up the chicken, broccoli, strawberry, and cup with the rose, and they all got in the car to go to the TV station. Dad made a phone call and arranged for them to meet their friend, the reporter.

When they got to the station, Mom and Dad's friend met them outside. He was very excited about the idea of using the food as spokespersons for water conservation. "What a terrific way to help everyone learn," he said.

He put his hand on his chin and thought for a moment. "Gloria, I have a favor to ask. Would it be all right if we planted you right here by the front door? You could be our beautiful, daily reminder to use water wisely around the station."

Gloria blushed, and agreed that it would be best if she were planted. Slurpy Ella was a little sad, but happy for her friend, too. Once Gloria was planted, Jackie gently rinsed out the cup, and then filled her with water.

Brian and Jackie worked with the director and helped set up the food and the cup on a table in front of a big camera. They practiced different

things they could say to help teach others how to use water wisely.

The kids told the reporter about Homer the hose, Scrub the shrub, and Blades the lawn. He talked to the director and they decided to take the camera outside and shoot some commercials out there, too.

"These commercials are really Public Service Announcements," the director explained. "Our television station cares about what goes on in our community. Conserving natural resources, like water, is important to our community. It's important to everyone!"

Mom put her arms around the twins. "I'm so proud of you both," she said. Jackie and Brian grinned.

"Uhh, HUH," Clucky cleared his throat.

"And we're proud of you guys," Jackie exclaimed.

"I'm proud of ALL of you," their dad smiled.

Brian nodded in agreement. "I just hope that these Public Service Announcements can help people learn about water conservation."

"I think they will," the reporter said. "And if it's okay with you, Slurpy Ella, Clucky, Chelsea, Bonito, and BonitaLita can all live here. That way we can keep doing announcements like this…and maybe even share them with other TV stations!"

Brian and Jackie were quick to agree that it was a wonderful plan. "What do you think, guys?" they asked the food and the cup.

Everyone cheered: "Yay!" "Hooray!" "Let's have some water to celebrate!"

And so they did.

The WeWrite Workshop was phenomenal!

The staff at Ewing created a wonderful atmosphere that helped everyone feel comfortable and creative.

We all learned more about water conservation, and had a lot of fun in the process!

All of the co-authors contributed, making this book
a true example of teamwork in action.

Leslie Andrade ~ age 8

"Most of all, I liked everything!"

PJ Chan ~ age 10

"I thought it was fun to be with all these kids and write the book and act it out."

56

Adam Favela ~ age 10

"I loved acting out the characters of the book."

Sydni Gethner ~ age 10

"It's pretty cool that we got to work together to write a real book!"

Mariah Gorham ~ age 8

"I liked being able to give my ideas. Everybody's ideas get used."

Maggie Gould ~ age 9

"I liked acting out the parts."

Nathan Gould ~ age 9

"I like to act. It was fun to come here!"

Daniel Levy ~ age 9 1/2

"My favorite part was acting out our ideas and coming up with ideas."

Ashley Paetow ~ age 10

"It was fun to be an author and to publish a book. It was fun getting to know people from other states and growing."

Austin Paetow ~ age 12

"I liked working with other kids to write this book."

60

Victor Serrato ~ age 8

"Acting out the story was my favorite part."

Harrison Trachman ~ age 8

"It was fun coming here. My favorite part was when we got to do the artwork for the back of the book."

61

Chloe Vicino ~ age 13

"I liked socializing with the kids and being able to write a book that's going to be published."

Sara Witzel ~ age 10

"I liked thinking about stuff the characters could say. It was really funny that Brian and the chicken leg didn't get along."

Allie York ~ age 10

"It was fun meeting the other kids and writing a real book."

Jack York ~ age 12

"Acting like the characters really helped us come up with what they might say in the book."

WATER
IS
PRECIOUS

So Plant a Plant that

is not too thirsty!

Xeriscape your Landscape

Lazy Daisy

Mexican Bush Sage

Barbados Cherry

African Iris

EWING

Irrigation ◊ Golf ◊ Industrial

Ewing Irrigation, Golf, and Industrial is pleased to welcome you to our extended network of family, friends, and landscape and irrigation professionals who are knowledgeable and dedicated to preserving one of the world's most precious resources.

We thank you for sharing some of your valuable time with us to learn more about the experiences of Brian and Jackie, and invite you to join us in our effort to help spread awareness of the global issue of water scarcity.

Our longstanding commitment to educating others about water management and conservation products is evident through close partnerships with key industry manufacturers, active involvement in industry conservation initiatives, and strong support of the Irrigation Association and the Irrigation Association Education Foundation.

Ewing is also a proud water conservation partner of the City of San Diego Water Department, and sponsor of the Annual Water Conservation Children's Art Program aimed at promoting water conservation through children's art.

Established in 1922, Ewing is proud to serve as your source for water management and conservation solutions. Ewing offers commercial and residential irrigation products, landscape and agronomic supplies, low-voltage lighting, erosion control, water features and industrial plastics to professionals serving the landscaping, turf, golf, and industrial industries.

For more information about Ewing Irrigation, visit Ewing on-line at www.ewing1.com.

WeWrite
BOOKS BY KIDS - FOR KIDS!

WeWrite, founded in 1993, is the publishing and marketing brainchild of Delores Palmer. The idea began in a public library near Springfield, Illinois, with an effort to encourage family and community participation in children's reading. It soon developed into "WeWrite Company," which conducts the creation of stories by groups of children of various ages. In a workshop, children, led by a professional facilitator and aided by an illustrator, are empowered to create, act, think, and dream. First, the children are introduced to the theme of the story through a tour or short presentation. Then they are given creative license to author their story, while an illustrator sketches their ideas. The end result is a published, educational book (or comic book) that is enjoyable for all ages.

Learn more about WeWrite Company on the web at www.wewrite.net.

Troy Freeman's career as an illustrator began right after graduating high school with the WeWrite Kids™ book *Coal Mine Scream.* He has worked on countless other projects with WeWrite since that time, and is always a hit with the kids.

The kids are a hit with Troy as well! He likes seeing their smiles and shares their pride and excitement when they see their ideas captured in pictures. When producing a book, Troy is a part of the team with the co-authors.

In addition to creating WeWrite books, Troy owns Dig•it•all Designs. Learn more about Troy's business at www.digitalldesigns.com. Dig•it•all Designs is dedicated to helping people achieve the visual presence they desire for their business. Our talent and services vary from web design, logo design, illustration, print, web hosting, and promotional advertising to mural painting, portrait work, commissioned fine arts, and airbrushing. With over 12 years of service Dig•it•all emphasizes superior customer service and design skills.

How the Co-Authors Conserve WATER:

I will turn off the hose when I take a break from watering the flowers.

Allie York

Nathan Gould

I don't take a bath, I take a shower.

Sydni Gethner

I don't hose down the driveway, I sweep it instead.

Ashley Paetow

I don't use too much water to water plants.

When you take a car to the car wash they use too much water, so we wash it at home because it saves water and money.

Chloe Vicino

Daniel Levy

I turn off the sink when I brush my teeth.

Leslie Andrade

I make sure my hose is not still on when I go inside.

PJ Chan

I try to take shorter showers.

Mariah Gorham

I take less time in the shower, and I turn off the water when I brush my teeth. Outside, I make sure that the hose is turned off.

Adam Favela

I turn off the faucet when I scrub my hands.

I don't keep the hose running when I'm finished watering. I also don't run water over certain areas.

Austin Paetow

Jack York

I look for more efficient ways to conserve water.

Harrison Trachman

I don't leave the hose on or anything else that wastes water when I'm not there.

When I'm helping my gardener I suggest things like using the hose after so you don't need to clean up twice.

Victor Serrato

Maggie Gould

I take short showers.

Sara Witzel

All the time that I brush my teeth I turn off the faucet, and when I wash my hair I only turn on enough water to get my hair wet.

68